P9-AZV-362

A READ-ALOUD STORYBOOK

Adapted by Lisa Ann Marsoli
Illustrated by the Disney Storybook Artists
Designed by Disney's Global Design Group

Random House New York

Copyright © 2003 Disney Enterprises, Inc. All rights reserved under International and
Pan-American Copyright Conventions. Published in the United States by Random House Children's Books, a division of
Random House, Inc., New York, and simultaneously in Canada by Random House of Canada Limited, Toronto, in conjunction
with Disney Enterprises, Inc. RANDOM HOUSE and colophon are registered trademarks of Random House, Inc.
Library of Congress Control Number: 2003106134 ISBN: 0-7364-2173-4

www.randomhouse.com/kids/disney

Printed in the United States of America

10 9 8 7 6 5 4 3

An Unlikely Totem

Sitka, Denahi, and Kenai were brothers. They lived a long time ago, when ice still covered much of the earth. The people of their village looked at the stars at night and saw magical lights that danced in the sky. They believed the lights were the spirits of people who had lived before them and now watched over them.

When it came to chores like hunting and fishing, though, Kenai's older brothers had to watch over him. Sitka and Denahi wished he would work more and play less!

But Kenai was excited. Today, he would receive his totem, a small animal carved in stone that would guide his actions. Later, when he learned to follow the ways of his totem, he would be allowed to add his handprint to the ceremonial cave wall, as the generations before him had.

"Your totem is love!" announced Tanana, the village elder, as she handed Kenai a small stone bear. "Let love guide your actions."

Kenai was disappointed. Sitka's totem was the eagle of leadership, and Denahi's was the wise wolf. Why couldn't his totem have been something important, too?

After the ceremony, the brothers went to get the basket of fish they had caught earlier that day. But almost all of the fish were gone! Kenai saw some bear tracks leading into the forest.

"Why is my totem a bear?" Kenai wondered angrily. "Bears don't love anyone!"

Instead of blaming the bear, Denahi accused Kenai of not tying the basket securely. Kenai grabbed his spear and headed off to find the bear.

Annoyed, Sitka glared at Denahi as Kenai raced away.

Sitka was worried about Kenai, so he and Denahi followed the boy into the forest. Within minutes, they heard a scream. Both brothers began to run toward the sound.

They found Kenai stuck on a dangerous ledge. Sitka leaned over the cliff and tried to grasp Kenai's outstretched hand.

"You've got to get out of here!" Kenai yelled, looking over his brother's shoulder. An enormous grizzly reared up behind Sitka.

Denahi tossed stones at the bear to help his brothers escape. The plan worked! But then the bear grazed Denahi with its paw, and Denahi fell through the ice. Kenai raced to help Denahi to safety while Sitka battled the bear. The huge animal knocked Sitka down, then barreled toward his brothers. Thinking they were in danger, Sitka summoned all his strength and drove his spear into a crack in the ice.

An enormous chunk of the ice fell off the side of the glacier. The bear—and Sitka—fell into the cold water below.

The bear escaped, but Sitka was gone. That night, there was a ceremony to say good-bye to Sitka. He would be joining the Great Spirits as an eagle. Tanana placed Sitka's spear, headdress, and eagle totem on the fire. Denahi sadly watched the smoke rising into the sky. But Kenai could feel nothing except anger.

"We're going after the bear," Kenai announced after the ceremony. "A man wouldn't just stand there and do nothing."

"Killing that bear won't make you a man," Denahi insisted. "Why can't you follow your totem?"

"You really think love has anything to do with being a man?" cried Kenai. He tore the carved stone bear from his neck and threw it into the fire.

As Kenai ran off, Tanana rescued the totem and gave it to Denahi. Denahi knew what he had to do. He put the totem in his pocket and raced away to stop Kenai, who was already far ahead of his brother.

Through the Eyes of a Bear

Kenai ran as fast as he could, stopping only to pick up clues to lead him to the bear. Finally he found the bear and chased it through a rocky canyon to the top of a high ridge. Boy and beast faced each other and began to battle. After a fierce struggle, the bear fell on Kenai just as he lifted his spear.

Kenai scrambled to his feet and looked down at the huge animal. Filled with anger, Kenai let out a cry.

Denahi heard the scream. He raced forward to find his brother.

Kenai looked up at the sky. Blinding shafts of light shone
down on him and the bear. Kenai tried to run, but wherever
he turned, light exploded around him. He pierced one of
the beams with his spear—then watched, amazed, as animal
spirits poured from the light and began to swirl around him.

"Sitka!" Kenai said suddenly.

Kenai stared in wonder as Sitka's eagle spirit swooped down in front of him.

Gently, Sitka lifted Kenai into the air. As the lights and spirits surrounded him, Kenai changed. He became a bear!

Denahi raced to the top of the mountain to find Kenai. Instead, he saw a bear standing next to Kenai's torn clothes and spear.

Suddenly a bolt of lightning struck the ground between them, and Kenai the bear was hurled backward over the cliff to the raging river below.

Denahi remembered what Kenai had said: "A man wouldn't just stand there and do nothing." Following his brother's wishes, Denahi tied Kenai's totem to his spear and prepared to hunt the bear. He didn't know it was really Kenai!

When Kenai finally washed up on the banks of the river, Tanana was waiting. Kenai tried speaking to her, but she couldn't understand him.

"I don't speak bear," she explained.

Bear? Kenai examined his reflection in the river and realized what had happened to him. He desperately tried to ask Tanana to help him turn back into a boy!

"Kenai, listen to me. Sitka did this," she said, trying to calm him. "If you want to change, take it up with your brother's spirit. You'll find him on the mountain where the lights touch the earth."

Tanana vanished before telling Kenai where the mountain was. He would have to find the place on his own. He made his way over to a pair of moose brothers named Rutt and Tuke to ask for help.

"Aaahhh!" screamed the moose. "Please don't eat us!"

Kenai tried to explain that he wasn't really a bear.

"Well, gee, eh," said Rutt, "you're one big beaver!"

Kenai gave up and walked away. He would find the mountain some other way.

Whoosh! Kenai stepped into a trap and suddenly was hanging upside down from a tree! As he struggled to free himself, a bear cub named Koda approached.

"You need to get down. Let me help," Koda offered, swinging a stick at Kenai.

"Ow! Stop that!" shouted Kenai. "I don't need some silly bear's help. I just need the stick." So Koda sat down and watched. And while he watched, Koda talked . . . and talked . . . and talked. Finally, after nearly a whole day had passed, Kenai agreed to let the cub help him. And he did. Kenai flew into the air and landed with a thud!

Moments later, Koda sniffed the air. He smelled something . . . something dangerous.

"Run!" the cub shouted as he took off into the woods.

Just then, Denahi emerged from behind a tree.

"You found me!" Kenai cried out in relief. "You wouldn't believe what a nightmare this has been!"

But all Denahi heard were growls . . . from his enemy, the bear. He raised his spear. Kenai quickly realized he was being hunted by his own brother!

Kenai ran until he spotted the ice cave where Koda was hiding. The pair sat motionless as Denahi walked across the ice above their heads.

Finally Denahi left. Koda asked Kenai to go with him to the big Salmon Run.

"I'm not taking you to any Salmon Run," Kenai said grumpily.

But Koda insisted, explaining that he had lost his mother and hoped to find her there. "C'mon!" he said. "There's lots of bears and a ton of fish, and every night we watch the lights touch the mountain!"

Kenai couldn't believe it! Koda was going to the very place Kenai wanted to find—the place where Kenai could speak to Sitka's spirit and change back into a human.

Koda was such a chatterbox that Kenai didn't know how long he would be able to stand him. But he decided he would do anything to get to the mountain where the lights touched the earth. He had to find a way to become human again. So, after a good night's sleep in the cave, Kenai and Koda were on their way.

Koda loved every minute of their long journey. He felt safe traveling with a big bear and started to look up to Kenai as an older brother.

Kenai wasn't exactly overjoyed about traveling with a pesky bear cub. But he had to admit that Koda could be fun every once in a while.

Along the way to the Salmon Run, Rutt and Tuke caught up with the bears. The moose had seen Denahi, and they hoped Kenai would protect them from the hunter.

"We lost the hunter back under the glacier," Kenai responded.

"So you don't think he'll follow those?" asked Rutt, looking at the bears' tracks.

"I've got an idea," Kenai said as he spotted some mammoths. He jumped onto a mammoth's back—just as he had when he was a human. Soon animals big and small were hitching rides.

The next day, Kenai and Koda stumbled upon an abandoned village. There they found a cave wall covered in tribal paintings. The handprints on the wall were just like the ones back in Kenai's village.

One painting showed a hunter and a bear. Kenai's heart filled with rage toward the grizzly as he remembered losing Sitka.

"Those monsters are really scary," Koda said, "especially with those sticks."

Kenai suddenly realized that Koda was talking about men, not bears.

The two continued their journey through the forest. Finally Koda ran up a hill and pointed at the Valley of Fire. It was filled with jagged cliffs and blasting steam. "The Salmon Run's not far," Koda said. "We just have to go through here."

Kenai and Koda began their scary trip through the valley. Suddenly a spear landed inches away from Kenai! It was Denahi— exhausted and bruised, but determined. Thinking quickly, Kenai plunged his claws into the ground. He made a hole that blasted a geyser of steam and caused his brother to fall backward.

Kenai snatched up Koda and headed for a log bridge that led across a deep gorge. It was the only way to escape.

As they were carefully making their way across, Denahi appeared and shook the bridge. Kenai lost his footing, and he and Koda dangled helplessly over the churning river below. Kenai struggled to pull them both up, then swung Koda to safety. But Denahi grabbed the log that held Kenai and shoved it over the side of the cliff with all his strength. Luckily, Kenai jumped off just in time!

Kenai and Denahi stared at each other across the wide ravine.

"What are you doing?" Koda asked Kenai. "We gotta get out of here!"

Turning to leave, they heard a hair-raising cry. Denahi was trying to leap across the ravine! Instead of making it to the other side, he fell and barely caught hold of the dangling log. Kenai watched helplessly as Denahi plunged into the river far below. Kenai waited and waited . . . until, at last, Denahi surfaced and grabbed on to the floating log. The bear heaved a sigh of relief.

Kenai and Koda continued toward the Salmon Run.

"Why do they hate us, Kenai?" Koda asked.

Kenai tried to explain that bears were dangerous, scary animals.
Koda didn't understand.

"But Kenai, *he* attacked *us*," Koda said. Both bears were getting
confused. In fact, Kenai was having a hard time remembering why
he hated bears so much.

Brotherhood

When Kenai and Koda finally arrived at the Salmon Run, a group of bears gathered to greet them. Koda was delighted. Kenai was terrified!

"Hey, Tug!" called Koda to a grizzly. "Have you seen my mom yet?"

"No, as a matter of fact, I haven't seen her," the big bear said.

Koda introduced Kenai to his friends. "He does a lot of weird stuff," he announced. "He's never sharpened his claws on a tree. He's never hibernated before. He—"

Kenai put his paw over Koda's mouth. Sometimes that cub talked too much!

Bears were all around Kenai—splashing, wrestling, fishing, and talking with one another. At first, Kenai didn't know what to think of this strange new place. He felt as if he didn't belong. But the other bears asked him to stay. Over time, he realized it was almost like a village . . . for bears.

With Koda as his guide, Kenai soon began to enjoy himself—even when he tumbled down a huge waterfall. Kenai was especially proud when he and Koda finally caught a salmon! By the end of the day, Kenai felt like one of the family.

After their long day of fishing, the bears shared stories about the adventures they had had that summer.

Koda told the story about the day he lost his mother. He described how his mother had told him to hide. Then he had watched her defend him from the "monsters" who backed her off the edge of a glacier into the icy water far below.

"She got out okay, but that's how we got separated," explained Koda.

Devastated, Kenai recognized the story from the day he had lost his brother Sitka. It was also the story of a mother bear protecting her cub!

Koda didn't see his friend again until the next morning. He pounced on Kenai playfully, but the older bear was sad.

"Koda, I did something very wrong," Kenai began. "Your mother is not coming."

The little bear's eyes filled with tears, and he ran from Kenai.

"I'm sorry, Koda," Kenai said, gazing down at the bear's small tracks in the snow. "I'm so sorry."

Kenai climbed to the spot where the lights touched the earth. He was going to ask the spirit of Sitka to change him back to his human form.

Denahi was waiting for him. He wasted no time in attacking. But Kenai would not fight his brother—that is, not until Koda suddenly appeared and jumped on top of Denahi. When Denahi turned on Koda, Kenai had to do something.

"Leave him alone!" yelled Kenai, running toward his brother.

Denahi pointed his spear at the charging bear.

As Denahi watched in disbelief, a large, glowing eagle lifted Kenai into the air. Seconds later, the bird set Kenai down. He was a human again! Just then the eagle changed into Sitka. For a few moments, the three brothers were together once more.

Koda cowered behind a rock.

"Don't be afraid. It's me," Kenai said softly. Koda ran into Kenai's arms.

When Sitka handed Kenai his bear totem, Kenai remembered the words Tanana had said to him when he had first received his bear totem: *Let love guide your actions*.

"He needs me," Kenai told Sitka and Denahi. Kenai wanted to become a bear again. His brothers understood.

Denahi placed Kenai's totem around his neck. "No matter what you choose, you'll always be my little brother," he said.

Sitka transformed Kenai back into a bear. Kenai turned to look for Koda. The cub had found his mother among the spirits. Koda and the spirit of his mother shared one last tender embrace.

Knowing that everything was going to be all right now, Koda went to his new brother, Kenai. With Denahi, they watched as Sitka and the mother bear returned to the beautiful sky above the mountain.

At last, Kenai understood the power of his totem. He had proved he could love all his brothers. Now there would be a paw print next to the human handprints on the villagers' cave wall. The prints would tell the story of brotherhood—and the love that connects all living things—to generations to come.